Kipper

Kipper's Toybox

Kipper's Birthday

Kipper and Roly

Kipper's Monster

Kipper's Beach Ball

Kipper's Snowy Day

Kipper's Christmas Eve

Kipper's A to Z

One Year with Kipper

First Kipper:

Colours Counting Opposites Weather

Kipper Storyboards:

Playtime! Miaow! Swing! Castle

Honk! Hisssss! Splosh! Butterfly

First published in hardback in 2008
by Hodder Children's Books.
This paperback edition published in 2009

Text and illustrations copyright © Mick Inkpen 2008

Hodder Children's Books
338 Euston Road, London, NW1 3BH

Hodder Children's Books Australia
Level 17/207 Kent Street, Sydney, NSW 2000

The right of Mick Inkpen to be identified as the author
and illustrator of this Work has been asserted by him in
accordance with the Copyright, Designs and Patents Act 1988.

A catalogue record of this book is
available from the British Library.

ISBN: 978 0 340 97045 4 (HB)
ISBN: 978 0 340 98847 3 (PB)

Printed in China

Hodder Children's Books is a
division of Hachette Children's Books.
An Hachette UK Company.
www.hachette.co.uk

Those bits are boring!

Hide me, Kipper!

Mick Inkpen

Hodder
Children's
Books

A division of Hachette Children's Books

Kipper was sitting on the first page of this book, wondering what sort of a book it would turn out to be, when a little squeaky mouse came running across the page.

'Are you in this story?'
said Kipper.

But the little squeaky mouse said nothing. It ran straight across the page and disappeared into the foldy bit in the middle of the book.

'I've been in lots of books,' said Kipper, 'but I've never been in there.'

'Go away!' whispered the little squeaky mouse from inside the foldy bit. 'Or he'll find me!'

'Who will find you?' said Kipper.

'Ssshh!' said the little squeaky mouse.

Kipper didn't see the cat arrive.

'Have you seen a little squeaky mouse?' it said. Kipper couldn't think what to say. So he just waggled his bottom from side to side until the cat went away.

The little squeaky mouse came out of its hiding place.

'He mustn't find me,' it said.

Kipper fetched his toybox.
'If he comes back, you
can hide in here,' said Kipper.
'He'll never find you in here.
It's always a complete mess.
I can never find anything...'

But the little squeaky
mouse wasn't listening.
It gave a SQUEAK!
And jumped straight
into the toybox.
The cat was coming back!

'I know you're here somewhere,' said the cat. He picked up Big Owl and sniffed. 'I'm going to find you, little squeaky mouse!'

'Is this what you're looking for?' said Kipper. He was pointing at something in the end of Sock Thing. A little bulge, the size of a mouse.

Kipper threw Sock Thing
which bounced tiny
bounces right across the page.
'There you are!' said the cat.
It chased after Sock Thing...
and pounced.
'Got you!' it said.

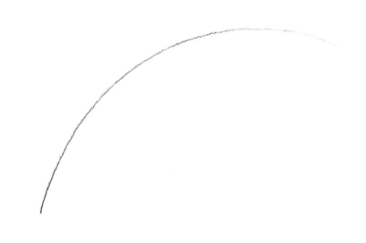

The cat held up Sock Thing and shook him.

'Out you come, little squeaky mouse,' it said.

Something blue and round plopped into the cat's paw.

It didn't look much like a mouse.

It didn't smell much like a mouse. It was Kipper's chewed-up old ball.

'He's coming back!' said the little squeaky mouse. 'Quick! Hide me somewhere else!' So Kipper grabbed the little squeaky mouse and popped it on top of his head. The little squeaky mouse folded itself in Kipper's ears. 'Look natural!' it whispered.

Kipper did not look very natural…

. . .he looked ridiculous.

'I know you're here somewhere,' said the cat. It sniffed the toybox. 'He's in here, isn't he?' Kipper shook his head, which was a **big** mistake.

'Found you!' said the cat.

Kipper grabbed the little squeaky mouse and ran as fast as he could, all the way to Big Hill.

'Don't worry!' panted Kipper, 'I won't let him get you!'

But just at the top of Big Hill Kipper tripped.

And fell!

And the little squeaky mouse popped out of his paws...

I wasn't worried actually.

. . . and went tumbling all the

. . .straight into
the paws of
you know who.
'Gotcha!' said
the cat.

way back down Big Hill. . .

'No! No! No!'
said Kipper.
'Please don't gobble him up!'
The cat looked at Kipper.
The little squeaky mouse
looked at Kipper.
And they both began
to laugh.

'Gobble me up?'

said the little squeaky mouse.
'He's not going to gobble me up!'
'Then why were you hiding?'
said Kipper.
'Because we're playing
HIDE-AND-SEEK, silly!'
said the cat.

'And it's my turn to look!' said the little squeaky mouse, jumping up and down.

'So it's our turn to hide!' said the cat to Kipper.

'So run and hide before I GOBBLE YOU UP!' said the little squeaky mouse.

And he could hardly count for giggling.

1 2 3 4

Just like the little squeaky mouse, Kipper squeezed himself into the foldy bit in the middle of the book.

But as you can see, Kipper is much bigger than the little squeaky mouse.

So I don't think it will take long to find him, do you?